Copyright © 1989 by bohem press – Zurich, Recklinghausen, Vienna
Published by Picture Book Studio, Saxonville, MA.
Distributed in Canada by Vanwell Publishing, St. Catharines, Ont.
All rights reserved.
Printed in Hong Kong.
10 9 8 7 6 5 4 3 2 1

Library of Congress Cataloging in Publication Data
Lobato, Arcadio.
Just one wish / written and illustrated by Arcadio Lobato
Summary: A magic crystal ball with the power of granting wishes destroys the tranquillity of a
small village, and only the shepherd boy who originally found it can save the day.
ISBN 0-88708-134-7
[1. Wishes–Fiction. 2. Magic–Fiction] I. Title.
PZ7.L7788Ju 1989
[E]–dc20   89-49263

Ask your bookseller for these other **Picture Book Studio** books by Arcadio Lobato:
The Greatest Treasure

Arcadio Lobato

JUST ONE WISH

Picture Book Studio

There was once a small village far to the south, a long way from any other towns. It was a poor village, so the people had to work hard. Even so, everyone helped each other, and it was a happy place to live.

As they went about their work each day, the grownups often stopped to chat with each other in the narrow streets. And in the shady gardens behind the houses, the children laughed and played.

Outside the village a young boy named Stephan lived with his grandmother. Every morning he set out with his flock of goats over the sunbaked hills to find food and water for them. And through the day, the people of the village could hear him playing his shepherd's flute.

Stephan liked his work, but best of all he liked the quiet evenings at home, for his grandmother loved to tell him stories and teach him about the stars.

One day up in the hills, Stephan saw a bright light shining from a clump of grass. There on the ground was a glowing crystal ball.

Carefully, he took the ball in his hands and turned it over and over. It was bright like a small fire, but it was cool and smooth like water in a stream.

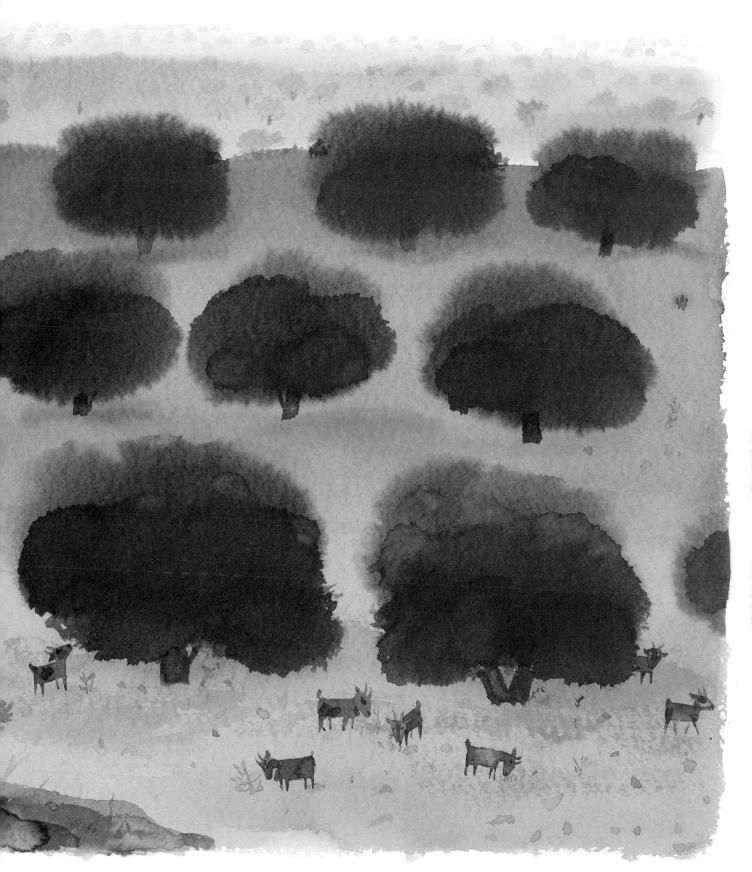

Suddenly he heard a low voice from inside the ball: "I shall grant you a wish, but only one," it whispered. "Whatever you wish will be fulfilled."

Stephan could hardly believe his ears. A wish! What should it be? So many things would be fun, but with just one wish, it must be something very special. Maybe he should learn to fly, . . . or perhaps sail on a ship across the oceans.

"I'll wait until tomorrow," he said to himself. "I need time to think about this."

He put the ball in his shepherd's bag, rounded up his goats and went home. And he kept his magic ball a secret.

The next day, it was just as hard to pick only one wish. Nothing seemed to be worth enough. Three days, four days— still no wish. Sometimes Stephan would take out the crystal ball and turn it over in his hands, and listen to the little voice.

But his days passed as always, and in the evenings, just like always, his grandmother told him stories and taught him about the stars. And Stephan was very happy.

In fact, Stephan was *so* happy, that some of the people in the village started wondering and whispering about him.

One day, a boy from the village followed Stephan out into the hills and hid himself behind an olive tree to watch.

He saw Stephan take something out of his bag and look at it for a long time.

The boy waited until Stephan fell asleep, and then he took the crystal ball from Stephan's pouch, and ran back to the village with it.

The boy called everyone together and showed them Stephan's crystal ball. The people were amazed, and passed the glowing ball from person to person. Then one man held it and turned it over and over in his hands. Suddenly they heard the voice offering him one wish.

Right away the man shouted, "I want to have a sack full of gold!"

His neighbor pulled the ball from his hands and yelled, "I want two huge boxes of jewels!"

The ball was grabbed and pushed and pulled from one person to the next. People wished for castles instead of huts, chests full of diamonds, cartloads of pearls, and bushels and barrels and barns filled with gold.

In minutes the simple village was changed into a grand city of great riches. Instead of old houses, there were beautiful palaces with golden doors. Instead of pushcarts and wheelbarrows, there were carriages and coaches. Everyone marveled at how rich they were, and people jumped for joy.

But soon there was trouble. The man who had wished for a sack of gold was jealous of the woman who had two sacks of jewels, and the lady with the jewels was jealous of the man who had asked for a castle.

People became suspicious and angry, and they didn't stop to talk with each other on the streets anymore.

And what about the children? No one had thought of wishing for things like gardens and parks and libraries and playgrounds, so there was no place to play and nowhere fun to go. Everyone was bored and sad.

In the evenings as Stephan walked home, the children looked down from the castles to see him skipping along behind his goats, and they could hear the sound of his flute. He was still so happy and cheerful. They all wondered, what beautiful thing had *he* wished for?

The children just had to know what Stephan had wished for, so they went out of the town to find him, and the grownups followed along, too.

They found Stephan near his house, and the little boy who had taken the ball from Stephan spoke first. "When we lived in our old village, we were all happy. Why did everything change?"

And the man who had made the first wish said, "What good are all of our palaces and jewels if we are not happy? Please, tell us what *you* wished for, Stephan."

"Me? I did not make any wish at all!" said Stephan. "But if you like, I think I can make a wish that will help to make everyone happy again."

"Yes! Yes!" cried the people, and the children clapped their hands.

So Stephan held the ball in his hands, and he said, "I wish that things would be the way they were before I found the crystal ball."

Everyone ran back to the village. There they found the comfortable little village that they used to live in—the same old houses, the same narrow, cheerful streets, and the same shady gardens blooming with flowers and trees.

Now the people of Stephan's village are happy again. They work hard, but they have their families and friends, and they have all that they need. The children play in the gardens again, and in the evenings the tender melodies of the shepherd's flute spread over the countryside like a smile.